Hugh McNulty

The Story Monster

Bumblebee Books
London

BUMBLEBEE PAPERBACK EDITION

Copyright © Hugh McNulty 2021

A CIP catalogue record for this title is
available from the British Library.

ISBN: 978-1-83934-301-8

Bumblebee Books is an imprint of
Olympia Publishers.

First Published in 2021

Bumblebee Books
Tallis House
2 Tallis Street
London
EC4Y 0AB

Printed in Great Britain

www.olympiapublishers.com

Dedication

For Darragh & Micheál.

In a small wee town
In a faraway place,
There was a funny looking monster
With a monkey's funny face.

He had a big hairy body
And some really shaggy clothes,
A rabbit's puffy tail
And an elephant's big long nose!

This monster wasn't scary
He would never give you a fright.
The only problem with him
Was that he hated stories at night.

He had a special power
When he made his fingers click,
He could make people speak gibberish
It was a really clever trick.

He could listen through a window
To hear a story start,
But once he clicked his fingers
He blew the story apart.

As children went to bed each night
He'd go from house to house,
They could never find him
He was quiet as mouse.

As Mummy tucked the boys in
She said, "Once upon a time…"
Then the monster clicked his fingers
And she said, "Snurgenburgenlurgenrime."

He giggled to himself
He thought it was so funny.
The boys never heard their bedtime story,
They just laughed at Mummy.

At the next house it was no different
As Daddy said, "A long time ago…"
Then the monster clicked his fingers
And he said, "Deet deet weet weet gogobo."

This happened every day,
Everyone was getting fed up.
All the grownups had a meeting,
How would they stop this cheeky pup?

"We should lock him in a prison cell."
"No we should chase him out of town."
Everyone was so furious
When a little girl said, "Everyone, please calm down."

"Has anyone tried talking to the monster?
We can ask if something is wrong?"
All the grownups laughed at her,
"Little girl get out, hurry, run along!"

The little girl walked home that day
But went a different way.
She went by the story monster's house
To see what he had to say.

"Please, Mr Story Monster,
Can we have our stories again?
I don't know why you're doing this
It's causing such a pain!"

He said, "No I just don't like them,
I much prefer my way.
It makes grownups sound silly
So, I'll keep taking their words away."

The little girl was flustered
Then she thought of something clever.
"Oh, Mr Monster, I'll tell you a story
It will be the best one ever."

He didn't look too happy
Actually, really rather cross.
"I'll click my fingers on you," he said,
"And your words will just get lost!"

"Once upon a time…" she said,
And his fingers raised to click.
"There was a baby story monster…"
She blurted out so quick!

He put his fingers down again
And heard her speak so clear.
A wonderful tale of story monsters,
He even shed a tear.

The monster, he was happy.
"Thank you, little girl," he said.
"I will not destroy your stories now
When you're all being put to bed."

"How can I repay you?
If you need me, I'm your man."
Then she had a great idea,
Another clever plan!

The next day after school
Her parents were giving out,
She hadn't done her homework yet
The grownups started to shout.

Outside, the story monster listened in
As her mummy said, "You are in big..."
Then the monsters clicked his fingers
And she said, "Foot doot root toot tig."

About the Author

This is my first published story. It started as a fun bedtime story for my two sons. They have great fun joining in with making silly noises and I hope other families can get the same enjoyment from my story.